THE GOOD-FOR-NOTHING PRINCE

Other books by Jay Williams

PHILBERT THE FEARFUL

THE QUESTION BOX

THE STOLEN ORACLE

THE COUNTERFEIT AFRICAN

THE SWORD AND THE SCYTHE

THE ROMAN MOON MYSTERY

THE MAGIC GATE

TOURNAMENT OF THE LIONS

MEDUSA'S HEAD

PUPPY PIE

I WISH I HAD ANOTHER NAME

LIFE IN THE MIDDLE AGES

BATTLE FOR THE ATLANTIC

KNIGHTS OF THE CRUSADES

JOAN OF ARC

THE DANNY DUNN BOOKS
(WITH RAYMOND ABRASHKIN)

THE
GOOD-FOR-NOTHING
PRINCE

by Jay Williams

Illustrated by Imero Gobbato

W · W · NORTON & COMPANY · INC · NEW YORK

THE GOOD-FOR-NOTHING PRINCE

King Baladin of Paladur was in a mighty rage, and it all began when he looked out of a window.

First, he gave a roar. Then he tore off his crown and stamped on it. That made him roar even louder because the sharp spikes hurt his foot. He gave the crown a kick, and hobbled over to sink down upon his throne.

"Guards!" he shouted. "Send me my high wizard!"

Soon, Talapic the wizard entered. He was called the high wizard because he lived in a room at the very top of the palace, and so when he came before the king he was out of breath.

"Yes, your majesty," he panted.

"Look out that window," commanded the king, "and tell me what you see."

Talapic did so. "Grass, trees, flowers," he droned, "a lake, a lawn chair, his highness Prince Palagon—"

"Stop right there," said the king. "His highness Prince Palagon," he said bitterly. "And what is the prince doing?"

"Why, nothing, your majesty," said Talapic in surprise.

"Exactly! *Right!* NOTHING!" The king's voice rose to a scream. "And what kind of prince is he if he does nothing?"

It was not absolutely true to say that Prince Palagon was doing nothing. He was, as a matter of fact, counting butterflies. He lay back in the canvas chair, smiling, his eyes half-closed. Every now and then a butterfly drifted past on the breeze. When one passed Palagon's face, the prince counted it. He had reached five.

He was a tall, handsome young man, every inch a prince. The only trouble was that he was lazy, gluttonous, and could neither read nor write.

King Baladin limped over to join the wizard at the window.

"Look at him," he grumbled. "The only exercise he takes is to get up out of one chair and move to another. Six or seven times a day he takes a long walk—as far as the dining room. He says he is too tired to do any studying, and so he cannot even read his own name. What sort of king will he make for Paladur when I am gone?"

"Not a very good one," Talapic admitted sadly.

"Correct. He must change," said the king. "And you are going to change him."

Talapic blinked. "Change him into what?" he asked.

"Not into anything," said the king. "You are going to change his mind about things, so that he becomes a proper prince. And if you fail," said King Baladin sourly, "I will have to hire a proper wizard."

Talapic took his magic wand out of his pocket. He was a little worried. In all his years of wizardry he had changed many things. He had changed a robber into a toad and a bird into a princess. He had changed an old shirt into a golden suit and a dragon into a worm. But he had never been forced to change anyone's mind.

He pointed his wand at the prince, and uttered a long spell in Old Magic. He was very nervous, and so he could hardly be blamed if some of the words came out wrong.

Prince Palagon disappeared, lawn chair and all.

"Well?" snapped the king. "What now?"

"Er—ah—um— that is only the first step," stammered Talapic. 'I must now go up to my room and begin on the second step. When I bring him back, all will be well."

He hurried up the stairs to the top of the castle and began feverishly searching through his magical books to see if he could find out what had happened.

Prince Palagon slowly realized that something was wrong. The sky had turned into a stone ceiling. There were no more butterflies. Instead, a charming and beautiful girl with long, brown hair was bending over him.

"At last!" she cried. "At last, you are here."

Palagon looked blankly at her. "I am?" he said. "Where is here?"

"Don't you know?" said the girl. "This is the Lonesome Tower."

The prince sat up. Sure enough, he was in a small room whose windows looked out above the branches of trees.

"I am the Princess Ola," said the girl. "And now you can rescue me."

Palagon sat down again. "Why?" he asked with a yawn.

"What do you mean, why?" said Ola. "I am being held prisoner by Sordilla the sorceress. You are a prince. You've *got* to rescue me."

"Well," said Palagon, "it's nice and quiet here. You have a lovely view. And you probably have meals served to you three times a day. Why leave?"

Ola frowned. "Because I am a princess. I have work to do. And my mother and father need me."

Palagon closed his eyes. "I'll think about it," he said.

Very shortly, the door opened. A tray of food quietly came in with no one carrying it. It settled on the table.

Ola seized it. With one swift movement, she threw it out the window.

"If you want to stay here," she said grimly to Palagon, "you may. But you won't get anything to eat."

Somewhat disturbed, Palagon tried to doze. He felt very strange. No one had ever treated him this way. From time to time, he opened one eye to peer at Ola. She sat in her armchair and said nothing.

Some time later, the door opened again. Once more, a tray of food floated in. At once, Ola snatched it and threw it out the window.

Palagon began to feel very uncomfortable. Something seemed to be wrong with his insides. Slowly, he realized that he was *hungry*.

He had never been hungry before. It was very unpleasant. It became so unpleasant that at last he said, "Very well. If you insist on being rescued, I'll rescue you. Let's go."

Quickly, Ola packed a small suitcase. "I'm ready," she said.

Now Palagon, in spite of his faults, was no fool. He saw from the window that the sides of the tower were too smooth for climbing. Turning to his lawn chair, he cut the canvas from it with his dagger. Being special canvas for a royal chair, it was very strong. He cut it into strips, tied them together, and soon had a tough but slender rope. He fastened one end to a chair.

"I'll go down first," he said, "so that if you fall you can fall on me."

"I'm not afraid," said Ola.

Down they climbed, one after the other. At the bottom, Palagon looked at Ola. Her cheeks were flushed from climbing, and her eyes sparkled.

"You are very brave," he said thoughtfully.

A thick forest grew about the tower. Together, they plunged into it.

For a long time, they walked. They pushed their way through bushes. Thorns scratched them. Branches caught at them. Then it began to grow dark.

Palagon said, "Perhaps we ought to rest."

"Not yet," said Ola. "We must get farther away from Sordilla's tower."

"You are very energetic," sighed Palagon. However, he found, as he went on, that he was not as tired as he thought he would be.

They came to a clearing as the moon was rising. By its light, Palagon gathered some wood and built a fire.

'I hate to mention this," he said, "but I wish you hadn't thrown all that food away."

Ola laughed. "Don't worry. I was prepared for escape," she said.

She opened her suitcase and took out two ham sandwiches and two apples.

"You are certainly very sensible," said Palagon. He grinned and bit into his sandwich.

Never had food tasted quite so good to him.

The forest was thick and gloomy beyond the fire. Mysterious rustles could be heard, the hooting of owls, the growling of strange beasts. Palagon put more wood on the blaze.

"Go to sleep," he said. "I'll stay awake and keep the fire going so that we'll be safe from wild animals."

"Let us take turns sleeping," Ola suggested. "Otherwise, in the morning, you'll be too tired to go on."

"You are very wise," said Palagon. "Very well. You sleep first and when the moon is halfway across the sky I'll wake you and take my turn at sleep."

She curled up under her cloak with her head on her suitcase. Looking at her, Palagon thought to himself, "I have never known anyone like her. And if she is brave, and sensible, and energetic, and wise, she is also very beautiful."

For all his good intentions, Palagon had very little practice in staying awake. He poked the fire and listened to the night noises. And suddenly, before he could stop them, his eyes closed and he was asleep.

He slept until the sun was high. And Ola, weary from the long march through the woods, slept too.

They were just waking when the witch arrived.

She came running through the woods. Every stamp of her great, flat feet made the ground shake. Her cloak flapped behind her like a crow's wings. She ground her terrible black teeth and laughed in anger. She rushed into the clearing and grabbed Ola by the wrist.

"Help!" cried the princess as she was dragged away.
Palagon, only half awake, struggled to his feet.

"Stop! Let her go!" he shouted.

"If you want her," Sordilla retorted, "you must come and get her."

And away she went, still clutching Ola, who struggled to free herself.

Only for an instant, Palagon hesitated. In that instant, the witch paused and waved her hand. Between herself and the prince rose a high, white hill.

Palagon tried to climb it. His feet sank deeply into it so that he could barely move. It was whipped cream.

A hill of whipped cream! Palagon forgot everything as he tasted it. Soft and sweet, it billowed around and above him.

Then he remembered Ola's unhappy face turned toward him as the witch dragged her off. Never before had the prince wanted anything except to sleep and eat, to be lazy and comfortable. Now, he wanted something for someone else: he wanted Ola to be safe.

He drew back, wondering how to get over the hill. He looked about and his eyes fell on Ola's suitcase. Since she had been prepared for escape, perhaps there was something in it that could help him. He threw it open.

He found a large ball of heavy cord. At once, he had an idea.

With his dagger, he cut two willow branches. He bent them into hoops and tied them tightly so they would stay that way. He knotted long pieces of cord over each of the hoops until, when he was done, he had a pair of rough snow-shoes. He tied them to his feet and up the hill he went—step over step, on the rich, thick whipped cream—and down the other side.

He took off the snowshoes. In the soft earth under the trees he could see the witch's huge, flat footprints. He began to run.

Ahead of him, he saw Sordilla pulling Ola along. The princess was doing her best to hang back. Palagon ran faster.

The witch stopped and waved her hand. At once, the air grew thick around Palagon. It was as if he were running under water.

He forced his way on, but slowly. The air clung to his legs and pressed against him. He grew tired. How easy it would be to lie down, to yawn, and to sleep as he had always done.

He saw Ola's face as she looked back at him. Never before had the prince wanted anything except to be left alone to do nothing. But now he wanted Ola.

He clenched his fists. On he went, fighting the heavy air. The sweat rolled down his face. Then, suddenly, the air grew light and thin again, so suddenly that he lost his balance and fell sprawling.

He sprang up and ran swiftly on. He drew closer and closer to the witch.

She whirled around to face him. She let go of Ola, who staggered and fell to the ground. Palagon sprang upon the witch and caught her by the neck.

There came a flash of lightning. It dazzled him. When he could see again, he found himself in a room with seven walls. In each wall was a door. But he still clung fast to Sordilla's neck.

He drew his dagger. "Set Ola free," he said, "or it will be the end of you."

The witch chuckled. "She is already free," she replied. "It is you who are a prisoner."

Palagon stared at her.

"I will be fair," said Sordilla. "Each of these doors is plainly marked with what is behind it. One of them will lead you out to freedom and the princess. The other six will lead you to destruction. You have only to read what is written on them."

Palagon let go of her. He gazed at the seven doors in dismay, for he could not even read his own name.

He walked slowly forward and put his hand on the handle of one door. DRAGON INSIDE, it said, but to him the words were just squiggles.

"Is this the one?" he asked himself.

He let go of the handle and turned to another door. This said, TIGERS HERE.

"If only I could read," Palagon groaned.

He looked from door to door.

"Oh!" he cried. "Why was I so foolish? Why did I waste so much time? Oh, me! Oh, dear, oh—"

As he spoke, he noticed that on one of the doors there was a letter that seemed to shape itself to what he was saying. It looked like a round mouth, saying "Oh."

"I wonder," said Palagon, "if it can *be* an O?"

He went closer and squinted at it. It did, indeed, look O-ish.

"This is a short word," he said. "Perhaps it says *Ola*."

"Well," he said, "I cannot stand here forever. I must just take a chance."

He seized the handle firmly and opened the door.

He was outside. There stood Ola, smiling at him in the sunshine. Behind him, with a shriek, Sordilla vanished and her tower with her.

Palagon and Ola set themselves to the long task of walking through the forest to the nearest town. There, they found horses and rode first to the kingdom of Ola's father.

They were met with great rejoicing, and soon they were
married. Then, with the king and queen and many courtiers
and soldiers, they rode to Paladur.

King Baladin welcomed his son and his new daughter-in-law with open arms. He looked his son up and down. Many adventures had given Palagon a bright and lively air. His eyes shone and his cheeks glowed.

"You are changed, my son," said King Baladin happily.

"And I remind you that it is all my doing," said Talapic the high wizard. He was even happier than the king, for since he had not been able to find out what had happened to the prince, he had been thinking of running away from home.

At dinner, the whole tale was told again for King Baladin.

"It was lucky, my boy," he said, "that not being able to read you were able to guess the right door."

"Tomorrow I will begin my lessons," Palagon replied. "But I will never forget the first word I ever learned—the name of my dear wife."

He smiled at her. "Although I cannot write," he said, "I remember the shapes of those letters, for they were very simple."

He dipped his finger in wine and traced three shapes on the palm of his other hand.

"There," he said. "OLA."

Ola put her hand over his. "No, my dear," she said. "You were luckier than you know. The word was OUT."

The Author

JAY WILLIAMS is the author of numerous books for children and adults. His books for young readers range from nonfiction (*Augustus Caesar* and *Knights of the Crusades*) to fiction stories such as *Philbert the Fearful, The Question Box, The Stolen Oracle,* and *The Sword and the Scythe.* Mr. Williams is also co-author with Raymond Abrashkin of the popular Danny Dunn science-fiction series. His stories, articles, and poems have appeared in such diverse publications as *The American Scholar, Esquire, The Saturday Evening Post,* and *Fantasy and Science Fiction.*

Mr. Williams served with the 65th Infantry during World War II and was wounded in Germany. In 1949, he was awarded a Guggenheim Fellowship.

A native of Buffalo, New York, Mr. Williams now makes his home in London, England. He is married and has a son and a daughter.

The Artist

IMERO GOBBATO was born in Milan, Italy, and received his education at the Royal Institute of Art in Venice. In addition to illustrating children's books, Mr. Gobbato has worked as a teacher, musician, art restorer, movie-set designer, and designer of sailing yachts. He enjoys painting seascapes and doing woodcuts and etchings, and has had exhibitions of his work in leading cities on three continents. Mr. Gobbato lives with his wife in Camden, Maine.

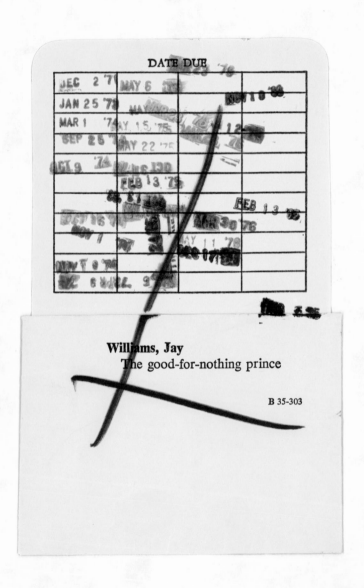